THE QUEEN'S PLATINUM JUBILEE CELEBRATION

2022

70 Years Anniversary

Kelvin Brooke

Copyright

Copyright©2022KelvinBrooke

Table of Contents

Introduction

Her Majesty the Queen will be the first British monarch to be honored with a Platinum Jubilee in 2022, after 70 years of service.

The Commonwealth will honor the Platinum Jubilee of Queen Elizabeth II in 2022, which will mark the 70th anniversary of her accession on February 6, 1952. On January 10, 2022, Buckingham Palace formally announced the celebration plans in their entirety.

Take part in the commemoration of Her Majesty's historic reign in the lead-up to the Platinum Jubilee Central Weekend, which will be held from June 2 to 5.

Dedication

Dedicated to all lovers of the Queen out there...

Chapter 1

Who Is Queen Elizabeth II

Queen Elizabeth II of England was made Queen in the year 1952, on February 6, and was also crowned on June 2, 1953. She is the mother of popular Prince Charles, who is the heir to the throne, and also the grandmother of Princes William and Harry, who are also very famous. She has endeavored to make her reign more modern and sympathetic to a changing public while upholding the crown's traditions as the longest-serving monarch in British history.

Early Life:

Formerly called Prince Albert, Duke of New York (later known as King George VI) and Queen Elizabeth Bowes-Lyon had a daughter named Princess Elizabeth Alexandra Mary, in the year 1926, on April 21, in London. Although most people had no idea that Elizabeth would one day become Queen of the United Kingdom when she was born. Elizabeth, often known as Lilibet, was able to enjoy her first decade of life without the stress of being the heir apparent. Elizabeth's parents split their time between a London home and Royal Lodge, the family's residence in Windsor Great Park. Tutors educated Elizabeth and Margaret, their younger sister, at home. French, mathematics, and history classes were offered, as well as dance, singing, and painting classes. Elizabeth and her sister were evacuated to Windsor Castle after the commencement of World War II in 1939.

In 1940, she made the first of her famous radio broadcasts, consoling British youngsters who had been evacuated from their homes and relatives. "In the end, everything will be fine; for God will care for us and give us victory and peace, "the 14-year-old princess assured them, displaying her calm and resolute demeanor.

Elizabeth began to take on additional public responsibilities shortly after. Elizabeth made her first ever public appearance in the year 1942, when her beloved father appointed her the colonel-in-chief of the Grenadier Guards. She started accompanying her parents on formal visits within the United Kingdom as well.

Elizabeth enlisted in the Auxiliary Territorial Service in the year 1945 to assist with the war. She studied to be a professional driver and mechanic alongside other British women. Although Elizabeth's voluntary job was limited to a few months, it gave her a look into a world other than the royal one. When she and Margaret were allowed to mingle anonymously among the citizens on Victory in Europe Day, she had another memorable experience outside of the monarchy.

Ascension to the Crown:

When Elizabeth's grandfather, George V, died in 1936, his eldest son, Edward VIII (Elizabeth's uncle), became King. Edward, on the other hand, was smitten by American divorcee Wallis Simpson and had to choose between the monarchy and his heart. Finally, Edward relinquished the kingdom to Simpson.

The event altered her life forever, making her the presumed heir to the British throne. In 1937, her father was anointed King George VI, retaining his father's surname of George. Her mother, Queen Elizabeth, was granted the title of Queen Mother, and her daughter, Queen Elizabeth II, was given the title of Queen after the death of King George in 1952.

Coronation:

Elizabeth was later crowned Queen Elizabeth II in the year 1953, on June 2nd, at Westminster Abbey when she was just 25 years old. On February 6, 1952, Elizabeth succeeded her father, King George VI, as king. For the first time ever, the coronation ceremony was broadcast live across the world, allowing for an unprecedented worldwide audience.

Husband Prince Philip:

Elizabeth married Philip Mountbatten (a surname taken from his mother's family) at Westminster Abbey in London on November 20, 1947. Elizabeth met Philip, Prince Andrew of Greece's son, when she was 13 years old. They remained in contact over the years and eventually fell in love.

Elizabeth was shy and reserved, while Philip was energetic and opinionated. While Mountbatten had ties to both the Danish and Greek royal families, her father, King George VI, was hesitant to marry her because he didn't have much money and was believed to have a gruff demeanor by others.

Her mother and Prime Minister Winston Churchill pushed for the family's name to be changed to Windsor, which annoyed her husband. The Queen reversed her decision in 1960, ordering her descendants who did not have royal titles (or who needed last names for legal purposes such as weddings) to take the surname Mountbatten-Windsor.

Over the years, Philip's off-the-cuff, incendiary comments and rumors about probable infidelities have produced a slew of public relations headaches. Philip eventually passed away on in April 9, 2021, at 99 years old.

Children:

Their son Charles was born a year after their wedding, and their daughter Anne was born in 1950. Elizabeth's sons, Andrew and Edward, were born in 1960 and 1964, respectively. By bestowing the title of Prince of Wales to Charles in 1969, she designated him her official successor.

When Charles was 32 years old, he married Diana Spencer (commonly known as Princess Diana) in 1981. His relatives allegedly coerced him into the marriage, according to later claims. The wedding brought massive crowds to London's streets, and millions watched the events on TV. The monarchy's popularity was particularly high at the time.

Grandchildren and Great-Grandchildren:

Prince William, the second-in-line to the throne after his own marriage in 2011, and Prince Harry, Elizabeth's grandson, were born to Charles and Diana in 1982 and 1984, respectively. Elizabeth has established herself as the adoring grandma of William and Harry. According to Prince William, she assisted and advised Prince William and Kate Middleton as they prepared for their 2011 wedding.

Williams, Elizabeth's grandchild, and Catherine, the Duchess of Cambridge, welcomed their first child, George Alexander Louis, on July 22, 2013, who will be known as "His Royal Highness Prince George of Cambridge" in the future.

The queen's fifth great-grandchild, Princess Charlotte Elizabeth Diana, was born on May 2, 2015, to William and Kate. Prince Louis Arthur Charles, their third child, was born on April 23, 2018. Prince Harry, Duke of Sussex, and his wife, Meghan Markle, welcomed the queen another great-grandchild to the queen with the birth of their son, Archie Harrison Mountbatten-Windsor, on May 6, 2019.

In addition to Prince William and Prince Harry, the queen has other grandchildren: Peter Phillips, Princess Beatrice of York, Princess Eugenie of York, Zara Tindall, Lady Louise Windsor, and James, Viscount Severn. She has 10 great-grandchildren as well.

Hobbies:

The queen has spent most of her time in the company of canines. She is well-known for her passion for corgis, having owned over 30 descendants of the first corgi she obtained as a teenager until the death of the last one, Willow, in 2018.

Elizabeth has a lengthy history with horses, having bred thoroughbreds and attending horse races. Elizabeth dislikes being the center of attention and prefers quiet pursuits. She enjoys reading mysteries, doing crossword puzzles, and even watching wrestling on TV, according to some.

Setbacks in Her Personal Life:

After the turn of the century, Elizabeth faced two big setbacks. She bid goodbye to both her sister Margaret and her mother in 2002, the same year she celebrated her Golden Jubilee, or 50th year on the throne. Margaret died in February after suffering a stroke. She was known for being more daring than other royals and for being forbidden from marrying a young love. The Queen Mother, Elizabeth's adored mother, died at Royal Lodge on March 30th, aged 101.

Queen Elizabeth's Diamond Jubilee, celebrating 60 years as monarch, was commemorated in 2012. Shirley Bassey, Paul McCartney, Tom Jones, Stevie Wonder, and Kylie Minogue performed as part of the jubilee celebrations on June 4th at a special BBC program. Elizabeth was surrounded by her family during this historic event, including her husband Philip, son Charles, and grandsons Harry and William.

On September 9, 2015, she surpassed her great-great-grandmother Queen Victoria as Britain's longest-reigning monarch, having reigned for 63 years.

Sapphire Jubilee:

The queen marked her 65th year of reign on February 6, 2017, making her the only British monarch to accomplish so. The anniversary of her late father's death falls on the same day. The queen chose to spend the day at Sandringham, her country estate north of London, where she sat in silence at a church service.

Royal gun salutes were fired in Green Park and at the Tower of London in London to mark the occasion. The Royal Mint has launched eight new commemorative coins to mark the Queen's Sapphire Jubilee.

Chapter 2

What is the Platinum Jubilee Celebration About

The Platinum Jubilee commemorates a monarch's reign of 70 years. The first British monarch to attain the milestone will be Queen Elizabeth II. On notable anniversaries, commemorations are held throughout the United Kingdom and the Commonwealth. This year, street festivities and public ceremonies such as the Trooping the Color, which commemorates the Queen's formal birthday, will take place. Public servants, such as members of the Armed Forces, emergency responders, and jail officers, will also receive a Platinum Jubilee medal.

What Date Is The Platinum Celebration:

The Platinum Jubilee happened on February 6, the anniversary of the Queen's accession to the throne when her father, George VI, died in 1952. The Queen customarily spends the February anniversary, or Accession Day, on the Sandringham estate in private thought, remembering her late father. She is, nevertheless, seen out and about on public engagements at milestone jubilees. That notwithstanding, Queen Elizabeth was crowned on June 2, 1953, at Westminster Abbey in London, UK. The big Platinum Jubilee celebrations will thus begin on Thursday, June 2, 2022, and will go through June 5, 2022.

When Would The Bank Holiday Commence:

An extra bank holiday has been announced for November 2020 to commemorate the Platinum Jubilee. The late May bank holiday will be moved to June 2 to make it a four-day weekend, and an additional one-off bank holiday will be created on June 3 to enable the celebrations to continue.

The Queen's Green Canopy Campaign

Members of the public are being asked to "plant a tree for the Jubilee," as part of a unique planting project created to honor Her Majesty's milestone. Individuals, villages, schools, businesses, and scout organizations are all being urged to participate in the planting season, which runs from October to March, in preparation for the annual celebrations. A total of 60,000 trees have been planted thus far.

In February, the National Trust announced that, in honor of the Queen's Platinum Jubilee, it would replant thousands of trees to rebuild Britain's lost landscapes. Planting pear trees to rebuild Rudyard Kipling's former garden, apple trees at Agatha Christie's holiday house, and 15 poplars to fulfill Harold and Vita Sackville-1932 West's vision of a tree avenue at Sissinghurst Castle Garden in Kent are among the 70 initiatives planned to commemorate the occasion.

Platinum Pudding Competition

The Jubilee organizers revealed in January 2022 that they were looking for a new national cuisine to commemorate the anniversary, similar to the Coronation Chicken, which was established for her Coronation in 1953. The Fortnum & Mason Platinum Pudding Competition is accessible to home cooks aged eight and up, and is judged by specialists including Dame Mary Berry and the Queen's personal head chef.

On Sunday, June 5, at the Big Jubilee Lunch, the winning pudding will be served. a nationwide network of community celebrations will be observed. There will be an extra bank holiday in the United Kingdom, and the customary spring bank holiday will be relocated from the end of May to the beginning of June to create a four-day Jubilee bank holiday weekend from Thursday, June 2 to Sunday, June 5.

The British government has promised a "once-in-a-generation event" that will blend the finest of British ceremonial splendour and pageantry with cutting-edge artistic and technological exhibits." This is the first time a platinum jubilee has been honored by a British monarch.

Other Commonwealth states and territories, including Australia, Canada, the Cayman Islands, New Zealand, and Papua New Guinea, have also announced plans to commemorate the Platinum Jubilee.

Chapter 3

Celebrations in the Commonwealth States

For the first time, Jubilee Beacons will be illuminated in every Commonwealth country's capital city to commemorate the Queen's 70-year. To mark the Queen's Platinum Jubilee year in 2022, the Queen's Baton for the 2022 Commonwealth Games has a platinum thread running the length of it. The Royal Mint and the Royal Canadian Mint collaborated to create a two-coin set to mark the Jubilee, with each mint creating a piece for the set.

The back of the silver coin, designed by the Regal Mint, features an equestrian picture of the Queen, while the obverse features a royal mantle. The reverse of the silver coin from the Royal Canadian Mint represents the Queen in 1952, while the obverse features the Queen's effigy, which has been featured on Canadian coins since 2003. To commemorate the Queen's Platinum Jubilee, members of the Royal Family will travel to Commonwealth countries on a series of royal excursions. The Queen's Platinum Jubilee Year was commemorated in Westminster Abbey on March 14 with a special focus on the role of service in the lives of people and communities around the Commonwealth.

Antigua and Barbuda:

The Earl and Countess of Wessex will visit Antigua and Barbuda in April to commemorate the Queen's Platinum Jubilee.

Australia:

Queen Elizabeth II is the first Australian monarch to reach the platinum jubilee milestone. To commemorate the Queen of Australia's 70 years on the throne, a number of national and community activities will be staged across the country. To commemorate the occasion, Australia issued commemorative stamps and coins. Monuments across the country will be lit, as will the Queen's Platinum Jubilee Beacon in Canberra. For hitting the milestone, Australians will be able to send a personal message to the Queen. Throughout 2022, events, activities, and festivities to commemorate Australia's Platinum Jubilee will be revealed.

Accession Day Events in Australia:

On the 70th anniversary of the Queen's accession, and the start of the Platinum Jubilee year, buildings, vice-regal houses, and monuments across Australia were lit in royal purple. Morrison and Governor-General David Hurley both issued statements to commemorate the Jubilee. Accession Day services were held in churches around Australia on February 6, 2022, to commemorate the Platinum Jubilee. The governor-general of Australia was present during a Festal Evensong at St Paul's Church, Manuka, in Canberra. A service to commemorate the Platinum Jubilee was held at Melbourne's St Paul's Cathedral, which was attended by the governor of Victoria.

A Choral Evensong to commemorate the Jubilee was held at All Saints Anglican Church in St Kilda, Victoria, with music from the Queen's coronation. A Choral Evensong was staged at St George's Cathedral in Perth, Western Australia, to honor the Platinum Jubilee. The governor of Western Australia was present at the occasion and gave a speech in which he paid honor to the Queen.

Platinum Jubilee Memorabilia:

To commemorate the Queen's Platinum Jubilee, Australia Post, the Perth Mint, and the Royal Australian Mint created commemorative souvenirs. To commemorate the Jubilee, Australia Post issued two commemorative stamps on April 5, 2022: a $1.10 stamp containing an image of the Queen painted by Dorothy Wilding in 1952, and a

$3.50 stamp featuring a photograph of the Queen taken in 2019. The stamp issuance was accompanied by a variety of collectibles. On April 5, 2022, the Perth Mint produced three commemorative coins to honor the Queen's 70th year as monarch of Australia. On one side, the shield of the royal coat of arms is depicted among floral emblems of England, Ireland, Scotland, and Australia; on the other, the Queen's first (1953) and current (2019) coin effigies are depicted.

Royal Tour:

From April 9 to 11, the Princess Royal traveled to Australia with her husband, Vice Admiral Sir Timothy Laurence, to commemorate the Queen's Platinum Jubilee. She began her adventure by opening the 200th Sydney Royal Easter Show, which she founded with her parents and brother Charles in 1970. She hadn't been to the event since 1988 till date.

Before attending a luncheon at Sydney Olympic Park, she served as patron of the Royal Agricultural Society of the Commonwealth. Representatives from the New South Wales Rural Fire Service, the Royal Australian Corps of Signals, and the Royal Australian Corps of Transport also paid the duo a visit.

Commemorations in June:

Buildings and monuments across Australia will be lighted in royal purple from June 2 to 5, 2022, to commemorate the Queen's Platinum Jubilee festivities. The Queen's Platinum Jubilee Beacon will be illuminated in Canberra on June 2nd, coinciding with other Commonwealth beacon lightings.

Bahamas:

The Queen's Platinum Jubilee was commemorated with the planting of two lignum vitae trees in Nassau's Retreat Garden National Park on January 28th. Crew members from HMS Medway and representatives of the Bahamas National Trust were among the guests of honor at the ceremony. On March 17, 2022, the Bahamas will mark the Queen's Platinum Jubilee by releasing a series of commemorative stamps.

Royal Tour:

The Duke and Duchess of Cambridge made a three-day trip to the Bahamas to honor the Queen's platinum jubilee from March 24 to 26. A world-famous junkanoo procession and the Bahamas Platinum Jubilee Sailing Regatta were two of the highlights of the couple's vacation in the Bahamas. Governor-General Sir Cornelius A. Smith hosted a reception on Cable Beach in Nassau for the Duke and Duchess of Cambridge on March 25, 2013.

Canada:

The Canadian federal government has organized a number of events to honor the Jubilee. Prime Minister Justin Trudeau had a virtual session with the Queen on June 11, 2021, during which they discussed plans for Canada's Platinum Jubilee festivities in 2022. In 2021, provincial governments began preparations for the Jubilee. Private organizations in Canada, such as the Rotary Club of Canada, are planning their own celebrations.

Royal Tour:

The couple will visit towns in Newfoundland and Labrador, the National Capital Region, and the Northwest Territories during their three-day journey.

Malta:

The Central Bank of Malta commissioned commemorative coins to mark the Queen's Platinum Jubilee. The Royal Dutch Mint produced the coins.

Chapter

Chapter 4

Other Tributes and Events

To commemorate the Jubilee, a Platinum Jubilee medal has been made. It will be given to persons who work in public service, such as military personnel, emergency responders, and prison guards. The Queen will bestow city title on several towns as part of the Platinum Jubilee Civic Honors. The competition received 39 applications. The Severn Bridge could be renamed in honor of the Queen's Jubilee in 2022, according to South Gloucestershire Council.

For the Platinum Jubilee in 2022, a statue of the Queen will be unveiled at York Minster. The two-meter-tall (6.6-foot-tall) monument will weigh around two tons. A new arch will be built to mark the Jubilee at the Princess Royal & Duke of Fife Memorial Park in Braemar.

To commemorate the Queen's Platinum Jubilee, Reading Buses unveiled a special bus with a unique livery. Throughout the year, the Platinum Jubilee bus will be spotted on the streets of

Reading, Windsor, and London. To commemorate the Jubilee, the Severn Valley Railway (SVR) has announced that its 34027 Taw Valley engine will be renamed "Elizabeth II" and painted purple. The new name was decided by a popular vote. By April, the engine will be painted, and after a few months, it will revert to its original green color. People from all across the world are being invited to learn and record a new arrangement of God Save the Queen, which will be delivered to the Queen. To commemorate the Platinum Jubilee, primary school children across the United Kingdom will get a free book in 2022.

The book will be commissioned by the British Government and will commemorate the United Kingdom's and Commonwealth's people, locations, and accomplishments over the last 70 years. The book will also look at the Queen's position and what the Platinum Jubilee means.

To commemorate the Queen's Platinum Jubilee year, GB News, a TV news broadcaster, announced that beginning January 18, 2022, the national anthem would be played at 5:59 a.m. every morning before broadcasting. The Platinum Champions Awards were introduced in March 2022 by the Duchess of Cornwall, the Royal Voluntary Service's president, to honor 70 volunteers nominated by the public for their work in improving lives in their communities. To commemorate the Queen's Platinum Jubilee, British Vogue featured her on the cover for the first time in its April issue. To commemorate the Queen's Platinum Jubilee, members of the Women's Institute crocheted toy corgis and hid them across the United Kingdom.

⬚ On the first day of the holiday, over 1,400 parading soldiers, 200 horses, and 400 musicians will come together to perform Trooping the Color in its entirety for the first time since the pandemic. The parade will conclude with the annual RAF fly-past, which will be seen from the Buckingham Palace balcony by the Queen, 95, and the Royal Family. On the day, the long custom of lighting beacons to commemorate royal jubilees, weddings, and coronations will be resumed.

The United Kingdom, Channel Islands, Isle of Man, UK Overseas Territories, and, for the first time, each of the Commonwealth countries' capital cities will be lit by beacons. The following day, a Thanksgiving Service will be conducted at St Paul's Cathedral, and the Queen will be accompanied by members of the Royal Family at the Derby, which will be hosted at Epsom Downs on Saturday.

The performers have yet to be announced, but it is expected to bring together some of the world's biggest entertainers to commemorate the Queen's most significant and happiest moments as monarch. On Sunday, a pageant combining street arts, theatre, music, circus, carnival, and costume will take place on the streets surrounding Buckingham Palace, involving approximately 5,000 individuals.

As part of the celebrations, communities across the country will sit down together for the Big Jubilee Lunch, where people will be welcomed to share friendship, food, and fun with their neighbors. The Queen is the first British monarch to achieve a Platinum Jubilee, having ascended to the throne at the age of 25 on February 6, 1952.

According to the palace, celebrations will take place across the United Kingdom, the Commonwealth, and around the world throughout next year, with the Queen and members of the Royal Family preparing a variety of engagements to celebrate the occasion.

The Prince of Wales, Duchess of Cornwall, Duke and Duchess of Cambridge, and other members of the Royal Family have yet to be named in the plans, but it is expected that they would attend various events.

Chapter 5

Summary

The Green Canopy program, which will grow trees to be delivered to the Queen at the end of the year, will be served alongside the dish as a lasting memento of the celebrations. Then, from the 12th to the 15th of May, a show in Windsor Castle will feature over 1,000 performers and 500 horses, bringing the audience on a journey through history from Elizabeth I to the present day

Proposed Plans for lengthy bank weekend holiday: A four-day bank holiday weekend begins on June 2nd, beginning with a ceremonial trooping the Color on Horse Guards Parade in downtown London. The UK, the Isle of Man, the Channel Islands, and its Overseas Territories will all light a beacon at the same time as one at Buckingham Palace on the same day.

The following day, a Thanksgiving ceremony will be conducted in the magnificent surroundings of St Paul's Cathedral, ahead of a star-studded Party at the Palace on 4 June. The performers for the performance have not yet been revealed, but it is expected to bring together some of the world's top names. Britons will be able to gather together for the Big Jubilee Lunch on Sunday, June 5th, which will commemorate the end of the bank holiday weekend. Balmoral and Sandringham, which are normally closed to the public, will be open to local residents during the holiday weekend.

In the Platinum Jubilee Pageant, volunteers, dancers, musicians, military people, and important workers will tell the tale of the Queen's 70 years on the reign, with a River Of Hope made up of 200 silk flags being paraded down the Mall. Additionally, schoolchildren will be participating, with the best being featured on the flags.

They have been tasked with creating a vision for the globe in the next 70 years. A trio of exhibits will be put on at royal palaces in July to commemorate the anniversary, as well as the Coronation and the Queen's several Jubilees.

Conclusion

We wish the queen a happy 70th jubilee celebration...